The Rainbow Zebra

By

Stephen Ayres
Angela Ayres

This book is dedicated to all children who have been bullied and made to feel badly for your uniqueness.

All inquiries should be addressed to:

Jumpboard Publishing
6514 Marlboro Pike #47743
District Heights, MD 20747-9997

The Rainbow Zebra/written by; Stephen Ayres & Angela Ayres

Illustrated by; Vivian Moore

ACKNOWLEDGEMENTS

We would like to acknowledge our family and friends who supported and encouraged us to see this project through.

A special thanks to Patricia Crews for her critique, proofreading, and non-relenting encouragement for us to complete this book.

A special thanks to Frances Daminabo for her critique, proofreading, and encouragement.

A special thanks to a dear friend Vivian Moore, who donated her time and artistic talent for the illustrations of this book.

Last, but not least a special thanks to Diana Woods a phenomenal college professor and meditation leader, who donated her editing talent to this book.

About The Authors

Stephen Ayres is a student at the University of Maryland Eastern Shore. He is majoring in English and Communications and has battled Attention Deficit Disorder (ADD) as well as a speech impediment of stuttering. He loves to write fan fiction, fish and is deeply devoted to his Christian faith. At eight years old, after being bullied at school, Stephen confided in his mother that his classmate's cruel words made him feel different as if he didn't belong. He felt singled out as if he was a rainbow zebra. Thus, began the inspiration for this book.

Angela Ayres is a graduate of Wilberforce University, a retired para-legal, and mother of two sons. She is very devoted to her family, loves to travel, write poetry and fiction. When her son Stephen told her how his classmates made him feel, her heart was broken. She too had been bullied as a child over 50 years ago.

The authors goal in writing this book is to reach and teach children about the hurt and pain associated with bullying. It is also their hope that if enough people stand up to bullying it will end. It is through the naïve and lovable character Rainbow, that they hope to achieve that goal.

ZEBRA FACTS

DID YOU KNOW?

1. Zebras have excellent hearing to listen for predators. They can twist their flexible ears in almost any direction to pick up sounds.

2. When zebras stand side by side, they usually face in opposite directions. This makes it possible for them to see in all directions and twice as easy to spot predators.

3. Zebra's early ancestors had three toes on each foot. Modern zebras have only one toe on each foot, surrounded by a hard hoof.

4. Many zebras have been killed for their beautiful skins.

5. All zebras seem to know when a lion is hungry and when it is just resting; they will often graze very peacefully when lions are around, but at a safe distance.

6. The eyes of a zebra are set high on the sides of its head to allow a wide range of vision. Even when bending down to graze, they can look out over the grass for predators.

7. No two zebras are exactly alike. Just as each person has his or her own fingerprint, each zebra has its own stripe pattern.

8. There are three different species of zebras; they are Plains zebra, Gravy's zebra and Mountain zebra and each species have its own special stripe pattern.

9. Zebras are social animals. They live in small family groups of 5 to 15.

10. If one zebra is in trouble, the others come to its rescue.

"Aw no!" Rainbow mumbled, as he heard his mother's voice awakening him from his dream.

"Rainbow, wake up! It is too nice of a day in the Serengeti to miss a moment of it. Look at that beautiful blue sky and sunrise. You love the sunrise."

"Not today," he thought. He wished he were still dreaming—then he would be running wild and free with the herd, even if only in his dream.

It was the same dream he had many times before, but today it felt real. He could feel himself running across the plains, the wind blowing through his thick blue mane and the heat of the sun's rays beaming on his back as he led the herd.

He so longed for the freedom of his older siblings, Leeko and Keela, and was getting tired of constantly being under his parents' watchful eyes. His blue, yellow and red stripes glistened in the morning sun as he paced back and forth deep in his thoughts.

"Rainbow! Stop pacing before you make yourself dizzy," said Mother. "What's wrong?"

"Nothing."

"Something is bothering you, so tell me what it is." Hearing her soft loving voice of concern gave him the courage to speak out.

"I want to run with the herd like Leeko and Keela," he blurted out.

"Rainbow," his mother sighed. "The time is not yet right."

She began to think back to the day Rainbow was born and the cruel words spoken of him. It seemed like yesterday; all the animals had gathered around to see the new addition to their family. When they saw him, there were loud gasps and looks of shock on their faces. They stepped back in horror as if they were in some type of danger.

"You should keep that thing hidden from sight until it rains; then others will think he's a walking rainbow," said Milton the monkey. The loud ear piercing "hee!" "hee!" "hee!" of Larry and Harry hyena still seemed to ring in her ears as she remembered seeing them rolling on their backs laughing and holding their bellies. Their high-pitched laughter echoed throughout the plains of the Serengeti. When they stopped laughing, Harry said, "You should give him to the hunters. He would make a pretty rug." Since that day, she and Rainbow's father always kept him close by, away from the herd. They never wanted him to hear the cruel words they had heard.

"Rainbow, as I told you before, you must wait until you are older."

"Keela was younger than I am now when she started running with the herd. Are you and Father keeping me from the herd because you are ashamed of me?"

"No, never!" Mother exclaimed. "We only want to protect you. We love you as you are and believe you are a special gift. You brighten our lives every day."

"With these bright stripes, I guess I do brighten your day," said Rainbow with a sly smile.

"At least you can joke about it." Mother said, as she nuzzled his head with hers. "Unfortunately, others don't see you as we do and are not very accepting of those that are different."

"Maybe if I were around the herd more, they would accept me as just another zebra, except with rainbow stripes. Anyway, I am too old to be with you and Father all the time."

"Rainbow, you don't understand how cruel they can be to those that look different."

"I'm a big boy now and I can handle whatever they have to say about me. Sticks and stones may break my bones, but words can never hurt me."

"I taught you that saying, but I was wrong. Words can hurt; cruel words hurt your spirit and make you feel unhappy. But you are right," she said with a sigh. "You are a big boy now. I'll talk to your father, and we'll tell you what we decide."

After dinner, Rainbow's father called a family meeting. "Rainbow asked to be allowed to run with the herd. After some serious thought and discussion, your mother and I have decided to honor Rainbow's request. We cannot shield him forever and must let him be free to experience life. However, you must always remember you are family, and family sticks together. If you leave together, you must return together."

Rainbow, Leeko and Keela were so excited that they could hardly sleep that night. They were so happy Rainbow would finally be joining them. "Beware of a zebra called Buck, and try to stay far away from him," said Leeko. "His parents named him Peewee because he is so small. He is a bully and is always starting fights. He got the nickname Buck because when he is in a fight he runs, bucks and kicks so fast and hard before you know what hit you."

"I can't wait until you meet my best friend Fay," said Keela. She is sooo cool and I just know she will like you."

Early the next morning Leeko, Keela and Rainbow went dashing out to join the herd. Rainbow ran fastest of all. "Slow down!" shouted Leeko and Keela.

"Come on, slowpokes," said Rainbow, as he ran even faster across the plains and up a hill where he stopped and waited for them. "Finally, my dream has come true, this is a happy day," Rainbow said to Leeko and Keela.

After they caught up with the herd, Rainbow's happiness quickly faded. The other zebras immediately began to tease him. "Hey! Rainbow boy. What are you doing out? It didn't rain!" Rainbow glanced down at the pint-sized zebra who had spoken those words and thought this must be Buck; all of the zebras, except Leeko and Keela, started to laugh.

"Why did you bring him along?!" Fay shouted in a demanding voice.

"He's my brother and I wanted him to come!" said Keela.

"We can't be friends anymore," said Fay.

"What do you mean, we can't be friends?"

"Your brother is a freak of nature. It ain't natural for a zebra's stripes to be blue, yellow and red. You can't expect me to put up with the likes of him; those stripes are too distracting and blinding."

"My brother is not a freak, and you'd better take back what you said about him!" shouted Keela.

Fay laughed in her face and said, "No way! You take your freak brother back!" Keela angrily pushed Fay down to the ground and raised her hoof to hit Fay but Rainbow stopped her.

"No! Don't fight over me, Keela. I can take anything they say about me. They are only words." But, inside Rainbow was hurt; his dream come true had quickly turned into a nightmare. Rainbow never thought the colors of his stripes would cause so much anger and fighting. They were treating him like he wasn't a zebra.

Buck shouted, "He does not belong here. He makes us an easy target for the hunters! His stripes can be seen a mile away." A tear rolled from the corner of Rainbow's left eye when they began to chant, "Go away! Go away! Don't come back another day!"

To his right, Leeko argued with Buck, and to his left, Keela argued with her best friend Fay. The taunts and jeers got louder and louder in his ears, and it was more than he could bear. "STOP!" He yelled to the top of his voice, and all fell silent around him. "I do not want to be anywhere I'm not wanted. I'm leaving."

"We're going too. We don't want to be where you are not welcome, either," said Leeko and Keela.

Rainbow, Leeko and Keela marched off together with their heads held high. "Don't pay them any attention, Rainbow. We don't need them. We have each other," said Keela.

"What on earth!?" said Leeko as the ground beneath them vibrated and shook. The thunderous loud roar of galloping hooves echoed throughout the plains.

"Wildfire!" "Wildfire!" was shouted by many. Panic struck the trio at the sight of frantic animals stampeding and running straight towards them. What had been a clear blue sky started turning black. Red flames flickered against a blackish-gray smoke-filled sky, blocking out the sun and turning the day into night.

Rainbow's stripes began to glow. Bright blue, yellow and red shined all around him, lighting a pathway. The animals stopped in their tracks, staring at Rainbow in shock and amazement. "You guys can tease me about my glowing stripes later, but right now, follow me to the river." The animals started running behind Rainbow, following the glow from his stripes.

They were beginning to cross the river when Rainbow heard cries of distress. "Help!" "Help!" "Please help us!" He realized others had fallen behind and he quickly turned, running back towards the sound of the cries for help.

"Where are you going?" asked Leeko and Keela.

"To lead the others that fell behind to the river."

"No!" Keela shouted. "You cannot risk your life for them. They don't even like you and they made fun of you."

"I cannot leave them behind—they need my help," said Rainbow.

"Then I'm going back with you," said Leeko.

"Me too," said Keela.

"Ok, but we must hurry. The fire is getting closer," said Rainbow.

Upon returning to the river's bank, they saw the smoke had started to become thicker and thicker. However, Rainbow's glow continued to provide light and direction to the river. "Watch out Rainbow there's a hole!" Leeko shouted, but the warning came too late for Rainbow. His right foreleg landed in the hole, causing him to twist his ankle and fall.

"You ok?" asked Leeko and Keela.

"I can't get up."

"We'll help you," said Leeko. They tried and tried to help Rainbow up, but his leg had been injured too badly.

"Go on ahead without me."

"No!" cried Keela. "Remember what Father said, we leave together, we return together."

"Father would understand why you had to leave me behind. You and Leeko must save yourselves. Cough! Cough!"

"We will not leave you here," cried Keela, tears streaming down her face. Despite their valiant efforts, Leeko and Keela were not able to get Rainbow up. The smoke started to enter their lungs, making each breath harder to take than the one before.

"You must leave me! The smoke and flames are too close," said Rainbow. The three began to cough uncontrollably, and they closed their eyes to shield them from the sting of the smoke. Leeko and Keela decided they must get help and frantically ran towards the voices echoing from the river.

"You had a close call," said a man to Rainbow, when he opened his eyes. Rainbow blinked his eyes twice, thinking, I must be dreaming. He had never seen a human up close before. Lots of animals and humans were all around, confusing him even more.

"Where am I?" he thought, "and where are Keela and Leeko?" He remembered being near the river's bank, the fire and then falling. The unfamiliar surroundings, the large area surrounded by a tall metal chain fence, puzzled him.

He spotted a familiar zebra walking towards him. "Oh no! It's Fay, Keela's best friend, or used to be until I came along," Rainbow thought. "She is the last thing I need to deal with. Now she's going to call me a glowing rainbow freak." Rainbow prepared himself to hear mean words. To his surprise Fay smiled at him. "Thank you," she said.

"What?" Rainbow said, not sure his ears were working right.

"Thank you for saving my life. You didn't have to come back and help us, especially after how badly we treated you."

"I went back because you needed help."

"I'm sorry, for being so mean to you." "How did you do that?"

"Do what?"

"Make your stripes glow."

"When I get scared or excited it just happens."

"You had better not be bothering my brother, especially after he saved your hide!" said Keela as she joined them.

"I was thanking him and telling him how sorry I am for the way I treated him."

"Keela! I'm so glad you are ok, said Rainbow. Where is Leeko?"

"He is sleeping behind that big boulder over there. What's that white thing on your leg?" Keela asked.

"I don't know, but I can walk on it now."

A zebra joins them and says... "Hi, I'm Kimba, welcome to the Serengeti Wildlife Reserve."

"It's a home for rescued animals. When the fire started spreading, the caretakers searched for animals needing help escaping the fire. Your sister and brother directed the caretakers to you, and they brought you over by boat across the river. They fixed your leg," said Kimba, pointing to the white cast on Rainbow's leg.

"You live here?" Keela asked.

"Yes, I was born here. The caretakers also rescued my parents from a wildfire some years ago. They were the only survivors of their herd." Kimba walked over to Rainbow and said..."The caretakers said you are a special zebra, unlike any other they have ever seen. I agree. You are unusual and beautiful."

"Thank you," said Rainbow with a big grin. Rainbow could hardly contain his happiness after hearing those kind words spoken about him and seeing; she accepted him and thought he was beautiful.

"Boy, am I glad you guys are ok," said Leeko as he joined the group.

People started to gather around Rainbow. One woman exclaimed, "He is the most beautiful zebra in the world. I must take some pictures right away."

Suddenly two adult zebras came running towards them. "It's Mother and Father!" Keela shouted excitedly.

"We're so glad you children are ok. You can't imagine how much fear we had for your safety," said mother.

"How did you get here?" Rainbow asked.

"We have no idea. I went to search for you when we smelled smoke and saw the flames from the wildfire. I told your mother to wait for us at home, but she followed me anyway."

"I could not wait at home while my children were in harm's way," said Mother.

"When we got across the river, the smoke was thick and we started choking and woke up here," said Father.

"We are so proud of you children. You are heroes. The story of your bravery is being talked about all over the reserve," said Mother.

"Rainbow is the real hero," said Leeko.

"You are all our heroes," said Father.

Rainbow was the star attraction of the wildlife reserve and was happy that others now knew what he had always known...It is ok to be different.

Made in the USA
Coppell, TX
26 December 2022

90700523R00017